Amber's Dressing-Up Dreams

The Diamond Tiara

JENNY OLDFIELD

Hodder
Children's
Books

A division of Hachette Children's Books

Printed and bound in Great Britain
by Clays Ltd, St Ives plc

The paper and board used in this paperback by Hodder Children's
Books are natural recyclable products made from wood grown
insustainable forests. The manufacturing processes conform to the
environmental regulations of the country of origin.

Hodder Children's Books
A division of Hachette Children's Books
338 Euston Rd, London NW1 3BH
An Hachette Livre UK company

1

"Girls, what did you do with my old gardening hat?" Amber's mum asked.

Lily, Pearl and Amber were watching TV.

"We took it down to the dressing-up box in the basement like you told us," Pearl replied.

"Did I really tell you to do that?" Amber's mum couldn't remember. "Well, I need it after all. Amber, can you fetch it

5

from the dressing-up box for me?"

"Later?" Amber pleaded. She wanted to watch her programme.

Her mum was ready to go out and garden. She stood in front of the telly. "Now," she said.

The three girls ran down to the basement and threw back the lid of Amber's dressing-up box.

"It's stuffed to the brim!" Lily exclaimed.

"Old shoes and boots, skirts, dresses, shawls . . .!" Pearl sighed.

"I know. It'll take ages to find Mum's hat," Amber grumbled.

"This is cool." Pearl picked out a cotton dress with zingy lemon stripes.

"Mum wore it to the beach when I was

6

two." Amber recognised it from the family photo album. "But hey, we're supposed to be looking for her gardening hat."

"I like this." Lily dipped into the box and picked out a shiny red shawl with a long fringe. She wrapped it round her shoulders.

"Hat!" Amber reminded them. At this rate they'd never catch the end of their TV programme.

Pearl dipped into the big box and held up a pink wedding hat with wonky feathers. "Is it this one?"

"Nope." Amber looked again. She pulled out a straw hat with a black band. It was crushed out of shape. "No, this was Dad's," she muttered.

"Let me try it!" Lily giggled as

she jammed it on her head.

"Do I suit this pink?" Pearl asked, trying on the wedding hat. She did a catwalk strut across the room.

Amber frowned and dug deep into the box. She chucked out one silver high-heeled shoe, a bent fairy wand and a long silk scarf.

Lily grabbed the wand. "Where are the wings?" she demanded. "There are fairy wings in here somewhere!"

"Hat!" Amber said crossly. It was no good – she would have to jump in the box and rummage in the bottom. She found the other silver shoe and a single white leather glove.

"Da-dah!" Pearl cried, leaning in and seizing a wide-brimmed cowboy hat. She chucked the wedding hat back into the box.

"Hey, cool!" Lily found what she had been looking for and strapped on some glittery wings.

Buried chin-deep in dressing-up clothes, Amber searched for her mum's gardening hat. She dragged an object to the surface – a dusty straw bonnet with a grubby white ribbon. *Is this it?* she wondered. And she tried it on.

"Ha-ha!" Fairy Lily laughed when she saw Amber in the old bonnet.

"No way would your mum wear that," Cowboy Pearl said.

Amber tried to take the hat off but something weird was happening. The hat was jammed on her head, she was

slipping down under the dressing-up clothes, amongst the silks, satins and sequins. And she could see a bright light at the bottom of the box.

"Amber, where are you?" Pearl ran to the box and peered in. A silver light shone. A cloud of golden glitter rose into the air.

11

Pearl's voice was faint. Amber sank down and down. She seemed to spin inside a cloud of silver and gold.

"Come back!" Pearl pleaded. ". . . A-a-m-ber, what about your mum's ha-a-a-t!"

Amber sank and spun until Pearl's voice faded into silence.

". . . The same as last time!" Lily shielded her eyes from the bright light. She had no idea what was happening – only that Amber's mum would be mad with her if they didn't go back with the hat.

Pearl turned to Lily with a helpless shrug. "Amber has played this trick on us before."

"I know," Lily groaned and threw down her fairy wand. The air was thick with

12

sparkling glitter. No Amber. No gardening hat. And Amber's mum's footsteps were coming down the stairs.

"She's vanished again," Pearl sighed. "And left us with a hu-u-u-ge problem!"

It was deep, dark night. The house was still except for the mice.

Amber sat in the cellar without moving.

Tick-tock. A clock in the wide marble hall ticked loudly. Mice scuttled inside the bare cupboards. There was a red glow from the cinders in the grate.

"It was the hat in the dressing-up box!" Amber muttered to herself. She should have known better this time around. She should never have put it on her head.

But here she was again, locked in the cold cellar. The whole house was asleep.

Tick-tock. Amber took off the old bonnet and put it on the table. She drew close to the embers of the dying fire. The cinders shifted and a small shower of orange sparks rose up the chimney.

Tick-tock. Tick-tock.

A grey mouse crept out of the cupboard. He ran across the floor and stopped at Amber's feet.

"Hey," Amber murmured. The mouse was cute, with his bright eyes and twitchy whiskers. She picked him up. "It's me again."

Another mouse appeared from out of a

dark corner, his little feet pattering over the stone floor. Then another. Soon Amber was surrounded by the tiny creatures.

"Are you locked in here too?" Amber whispered. "Don't they leave you any scraps?"

She'd left behind her home and the

dressing-up box in the basement. She'd travelled through the bright, glittering light into the house of the Uglies and the dreaded stepmother, Octavia. She was slap-bang back in Cinderella world.

"Aah, you're hungry!" Amber said to her mouse mates.

Tick-tock. The clock in the hall measured the long, lonely night. The mice scampered across her lap.

"I know where there's something to eat!" Amber declared, getting up and going to one of the cupboards. She remembered the sugar-mice Buttons had given her during her first visit.

"Here," she told the real mice, breaking a sweet treat into small pieces.

The mice nibbled happily.

"Buttons is the only cool person around here," Amber sighed. "Once he realised I was trying to run away, he let me hide in his gran's house."

The mice's sharp teeth chomped on the sugar. *Tick-tock* went the clock.

"Cin-der-ell-a!" a voice screamed suddenly.

Amber jumped up with fright. The mice scattered into the shadows.

"Cinderella, wake up!" Louisa cried from the top of the house. Her shrill voice carried along the corridors, down into the cellar. "I can't sleep!"

So? Amber thought. *What am I supposed to do – wave a magic wand?*

"Cin-der-ell-a!" Charlotte's loud voice joined in.

"Lazy girl, where are you?" Louisa demanded. "Come upstairs at once!"

Someone will have to open this cellar door first, Amber thought as she went up the stone steps. She tried the handle – just as she thought; the door was locked.

Then she heard footsteps. A key turned in the lock and Charlotte appeared, candle in hand.

"We wouldn't have to lock you in if you didn't try to run away all the time," Charlotte whined. She yawned and rubbed her eyes. "And then I wouldn't have to get out of bed when I needed you in the middle of the night."

So you don't look any better than when I last saw you, Amber thought, ignoring Charlotte's complaints. *The same tall, stringy beanpole. Curlers in her hair, thick face-cream.*

"Louisa woke me from my beauty sleep," Charlotte groaned. "And now I shall look a fright for the Prince's Ball tomorrow."

Yeah! Amber thought. *No argument there.*

"What do you want?" she asked abruptly.

She couldn't even pretend to be nice to the Uglies.

"Hot chocolate," Charlotte snapped.

"Make that two," Louisa added, appearing at the far end of the hallway.

She slip-slopped towards Charlotte and Amber in her fluffy slippers, her long white nightgown stopping short of her chubby ankles. "But make mine extra-large, with five spoons of sugar and lots of extra chocolate sprinkled on top!"

3

Amber boiled milk in a pan over the low fire and added the chocolate and sugar. Then she carried the steaming mugs on a tray along the dark corridor and up the wide stairs.

"They're so mean they don't even give me a candle to light my way," Amber grumbled to herself as she passed by Octavia's doorway.

The Diamond Tiara

A breeze blew down the corridor and slammed a door. Tapestries billowed away from the wall. Everywhere there were shadows and dark turnings. The wind seemed to whisper a warning.

"At last!" Louisa shrieked as Amber arrived with her hot drink. She sipped it then spat it out. "Too much sugar!" she cried.

"But you told me five teaspoons," Amber objected.

"Yuck!" Louisa flung the mug on to the floor. "Go away, you useless wretch!"

Taking a deep breath, Amber went on to Charlotte's room. The light was off and there was a loud sound of snoring coming from the bed. Charlotte was fast asleep.

Typical! Amber tiptoed forward and left the drink to go cold on the bedside table. Then she backed out and quietly closed the door.

"Cinderella, come back in here!" Louisa demanded as Amber tried to slip past her room. "I can hear you creeping around, so there's no use pretending you're not there."

Sighing, Amber did as she was told.

Louisa started in on her the moment she set foot inside the door. "Why must you always look so mean and spiteful?" she demanded. "Would it be too much to expect a smile?"

"Me?" Amber retorted. Louisa was the champion scowler around here. Her round face was always twisted into a furious frown.

Louisa stopped Amber in her tracks. "My curlers are coming out where I lay on them. You must put them back in."

Silently Amber obeyed, though she knew no amount of curling would make Louisa look good for the Ball next day.

"Ouch!" Louisa scowled and smacked Amber's hand. "Don't be so rough, you clumsy thing!"

Outside the room, the breeze still tugged at the tapestries. Another door banged shut. Then Amber thought she heard footsteps.

"Watch what you're doing!" Louisa snapped, snatching a curler from Amber. "Oh, for heaven's sake, I'll do it myself!"

"Are you sure?" At that moment, with the creaks and noises out in the corridor, Amber would rather have stayed.

Louisa wound her dark hair around the curler. "Yes, get out!"

So Amber left the room, her heart beating fast. Was it the wind slamming the doors, or was it an intruder? She tiptoed down the corridor, past Octavia's open door.

". . . Now is the time," Octavia muttered urgently to a figure dressed in a black cloak. "Here is the key to the cellar.

Before the clock strikes midnight, you must kidnap Cinderella!"

Amber gasped and felt her knees go weak. Of course – wicked old Octavia was planning to get rid of her once and for all! How could Amber have forgotten?

"You will take her out of the city to the forest on the mountain," Octavia instructed. "Then leave her there."

The man in the cloak muttered under his breath.

No way! Amber thought. Getting over her shock, she began to run.

Just then the clock in the hall began to chime. *One-two-three.* Amber gathered up her long skirt and fled down the marble steps. She must hide, but where?

Four-five-six. The dark stranger left

28

Octavia's room, spotted Amber and followed her down the stairs.

Seven-eight-nine. Each stroke chilled Amber to the bone. She must hide here – behind a tapestry, hoping that the kidnapper would pass by.

Ten-eleven-twelve. Midnight. The man's footsteps drew near. He paused, then went on.

Behind the musty, dusty tapestry Amber breathed a sigh of relief.

The kidnapper stopped and listened hard. He turned to retrace his steps.

Aaa-choo! The dust got up Amber's nose.

The man heard the sneeze then saw Amber's bare feet sticking out from underneath the tapestry.

Help! Save me! Amber thought. She

didn't cry out because there was only Cinderella's deaf old father upstairs in his room, and he would be fast asleep.

The kidnapper pulled the tapestry from its wooden pole and brought it crashing down on Amber. She yelled and struggled.

"Keep still!" He wrestled with Amber and the heavy tapestry.

She wriggled free and saw the man get tangled up. It gave her a few extra seconds to get away.

Amber ran again. The man sprang free and followed her back down the hall, up the stairs, along the dark corridor.

"Father, wake up!" she cried, hammering at the old man's door. "They are trying to kidnap me! Wake up. Father, help me!"

4

Amber waited for the old man's doddery footsteps. She put her ear to his bedroom door, praying that he had heard.

Meanwhile her kidnapper ducked out of the corridor into Octavia's room.

"Father!" Amber cried again. "Send for the soldiers! Quickly, before it's too late!"

But the deaf old man snoozed on.

And soon Octavia flew out of her room,

her face purple with fury. "Little nuisance!" she snapped, seizing Amber and hauling her down the stairs. "You are the bane of my life, Cinderella. But soon I shall be rid of you for ever!"

"For ever!" Charlotte and Louisa echoed as they rushed from their rooms and leaned over the banister.

"And you three are wicked, wicked, wicked!" Amber cried. She kicked and wriggled to get free.

"We will be rid of you and it will be as if you never lived!" Octavia hissed, looking up the stairway for her cloaked accomplice.

"Oh no you don't. It's not that easy!" Amber said, lunging forward and taking a hard bite at Octavia's wrist.

"Aaargh!" Octavia shrieked and let go.

Amber fled again, this time towards the big front door. She threw herself against it to force it open, but only winded herself and fell back on to the floor.

As she slumped forward to catch her breath, she heard Louisa and Charlotte charge down the stairs.

"Catch her!" Charlotte yelled.

"Sit on her!" Louisa cried.

They jumped on Amber, sat on her hard and squished her with their weight. And though Amber struggled as hard as she could, she could not budge the Uglies.

*

"Take her away." Octavia nursed her sore wrist as she gave her stern order to the kidnapper.

The sly man had shown up when the fight was over, ready to haul Amber off to the forest.

"Is your horse waiting outside?" Octavia checked as she took a big key from the bunch hanging from her waist and unlocked the door.

The kidnapper nodded.

As the Uglies dragged Amber to her feet, she noticed that the man wore long riding boots with spurs and a broad-brimmed hat which hid his lean face.

"Ready?" Octavia checked again.

"Ready!" he growled.

And before Amber could resist, the door

was flung open, the man seized her around the waist and hoisted her on to a grey horse.

He slung her across the front of the saddle and leaped up behind. Then he kicked with his spurs and they were off, along the broad street, hooves clattering,

iron shoes sending up bright sparks as they raced away.

"Good riddance!" Charlotte cried after them.

"Yes, good riddance to a lazy, spiteful girl!" Louisa agreed, slamming the door and going back to bed.

5

The grey horse galloped through the town.

The houses were shuttered. People were fast asleep.

"Who goes there?" a guard asked at the foot of the winding steps leading to the Prince's Palace on the hill.

The kidnapper reined back, swerved and headed off down a narrow street. The horse raced on.

"Help!" Amber cried. She was slung like a parcel across the front of the saddle, bouncing and bumping, clinging on for dear life.

The man spurred his horse over the old stone bridge, then up more alleys. Soon they would reach the edge of the town.

"Help!" Amber cried again. She thought she recognised the tiny street where Buttons lived with his grandmother. They passed by with a clatter of hooves.

Inside one of the houses, a light went on and a face appeared at an upstairs window.

Then there were no more streets, no more houses – only a track leading up the mountain towards a dark forest.

And still Amber had to cling on as the

grey mare galloped up the hill.

They came to the trees and the horse slowed. She picked her way between stout trunks, under low-hanging branches.

Now her hooves fell softly on the dead leaves underfoot. She swished through bushes, jumped fallen logs and trotted on.

"Please stop!" Amber said to the kidnapper. Her ribs ached so much she could hardly breathe.

But the man urged his horse on into the forest. He only slowed to a walk when the mare was covered in sweat and could run no further.

Twisting round, Amber could make out a tangle of branches above and trees all around, standing straight as sentries, blocking their way. "Don't leave me here!"

she pleaded as the man brought his horse to a halt.

"It's what I'm paid to do," he answered gruffly, pushing Amber from the saddle.

She fell to the ground. "Wait! You can't be that mean!"

"Like I said before – it's a job," he told her coldly.

Amber picked herself up. "But it's dark. I'm lost. I'm never going to find my way out of here!"

The black-hearted kidnapper nodded and reined his horse round.

The mare reared up. Her mane flashed white under a glimmer of moonlight. Then, without another word, her rider touched her with his spurs and she set off at a gallop.

"Come back!" Amber cried.

But horse and rider galloped off through the dark forest.

Amber stood in the thick silence. She took a step to follow the kidnapper, then another. But it was too dark to see his tracks.

I will sit here until it gets light, she decided, tucking her skirt around her legs and drawing her knees up to her chin. *In the morning I will be able to find my way.*

"Tu-woo! Tu-woo!" An owl hooted and a white shape glided overhead.

Amber shivered. *It's only an owl*, she told herself.

In some bushes close by, she heard a creature stir.

Probably a rabbit, Amber decided. *At the very worst, a fox!*

The night was black and thick and silent. Amber sat and shivered.

"Ow-wooo! Ow-woooo!" A wild animal howled in the darkness.

"That was no rabbit or fox!" Amber jumped to her feet. The sound carried through the forest, making the hairs at the back of her neck stand on end.

"Ow-wooooo!"

"That's a wolf – and I'm out of here!"

Amber ran through the trees. She tripped over roots and blundered into bushes. Thorns scratched her, branches caught in her hair.

She ran until she was tired and her legs would run no further. Then she sank to the ground.

Bright eyes stared at her from the undergrowth. A creature growled.

"Oh!" Amber gasped. It was the wolf. It had followed her and was staring at her with hungry eyes.

Leaves rustled, a twig snapped. The creature crept nearer.

Amber dragged herself to her feet. Wearily she tried to run again.

But the creature followed. She could hear his breath though she couldn't see him. He seemed to outpace her, so that now the sounds came from in front – twigs breaking, hot breath panting, a large shape breaking through the bushes into a clearing ahead.

In the moonlight she saw those eyes – bright and gleaming. Then his floppy ears, pink tongue and long, shaggy coat . . . Wait a minute, this was no wolf . . .

The creature padded out into the clearing. He wagged his tail and trotted towards Amber.

"It's a dog!" she cried.

A big, shaggy brown and white dog with a collar, which meant he belonged to somebody. And he was coming towards her and sitting so she could stroke him.

He was so big that he came up to her chest even when he sat and put his big head close to her and kept on wagging his long, bushy tail.

6

"Am I glad to see you!" Amber told the shaggy St Bernard.

The dog cosied up and let himself be stroked. He allowed Amber to read the name on the disc hanging from his collar.

"'Bruno'," Amber read. "So, Bruno, you have to get me out of this mess. Take me to your owner. Go ahead – lead the way!"

"Woof!" The bark was deep and scary

but Bruno seemed to understand. He stood up and trotted out of the clearing, back into the dark forest.

Am I crazy? Amber thought. *Here am I, trusting my life to a shaggy dog who I only just met. He already scared me half to death, and now I'm following him into the thickest, darkest forest!*

"Ow-woooo!" a wolf howled from the depths of the forest.

"Woof!" friendly Bruno barked.

Amber shot into the forest after him. "What do I have to lose?" she muttered. But then fresh fears took hold of her. "What if Bruno takes me round in circles, or worse still, deeper into the forest?"

The dog padded onwards without looking back.

"He seems to know what he's doing." Amber took a deep breath and kept on following. "OK, show me the way out of here," she said.

The big dog walked silently through the night.

Once in a while he turned his head to make sure that Amber was following.

"I'm coming!" she would gasp, pushing her way through thick undergrowth.

Twice Bruno stopped to let Amber rest.

"I'm so tired!" she sighed, propping herself against a thick trunk and tilting her head to look up at the moon. "My ribs ache and my legs won't carry me much further."

In the distance, the sound of wolves

howling made her shiver and stand up again. "Let's go!" she urged. "Come on, Bruno, lead the way."

At last it grew light. There was a pink glow in the eastern sky. Slowly the darkness lifted.

Not far now! Bruno seemed to tell Amber as he turned his head and gave a deep bark.

But where had he brought her? In the dim grey light Amber gazed around. They were still deep in the forest, surrounded by trees. "Ah," she sighed wearily with a shake of her head.

"Woof!" Bruno insisted. He led the way into another opening in the forest with a log pile and a small stream. And at the far edge of the frosty clearing was a small, neat cottage with smoke curling from its chimney.

*

"Bruno saved my life!" Amber sat at the cottage table drinking warm milk and eating fresh bread and ham. "He rescued me from the wolves and led me here."

A kindly woman called Betty stood opposite. She was dressed in a big, plain apron and a long flowered dress. "Eat your breakfast," Betty urged. "Save your story for later."

Betty had heard Bruno's bark and appeared at the door. The moment she'd seen Amber she'd rushed forward and invited her in, fussed over her and sat her down to eat.

"Catch your breath," Betty said now, studying Amber carefully. "And when you have regained your strength, tell me how you came to be lost in the forest."

"Your dog is so cool!" Amber changed the subject and tried to work out what to do next.

Bruno sat next to her, waiting patiently for her to sneak him a chunk of ham from her plate.

Betty smiled. "My husband, Jack, is a woodcutter," she told Amber. "He sends logs to the Prince himself, to light fires in the great palace. He is there now, delivering wood for the Prince's Ball."

"Tonight," Amber nodded.

"Jack will stay in town to see the streets lit with great flaming torches for the party. The Prince says anyone may join in and watch the fireworks at midnight."

Bruno wagged his tail and snaffled the scrap which Amber offered him.

"How come Bruno was out in the forest last night?" she asked.

Betty stood, hands on hips. "Answer my question first. How did you get lost?"

"Wait, I can't talk with my mouth full," Amber mumbled.

"Very well." Betty was kindly but firm. "I will ask you a question and you need only nod or shake your head. Firstly your name – does it begin with the letter 'C'?"

Amber frowned.

"And is the 'C' followed by an 'I' and an 'N' and a 'D'?"

"Stop!" Amber cried. She jumped up from the table. "How do you know my name?"

"My nephew was right – you're Cinderella!" Betty exclaimed. "You galloped from the town on a grey mare. There was a man in a black cloak . . ."

Amber shook her head and ran to the cottage door. Somehow, somewhere, someone had betrayed her. She rushed outside.

"'Here we go round the mulberry bush,'" a voice sang. "'The mulberry bush, the mulberry bush . . .'"

A figure was perched on the log pile wearing a long red scarf and a cap pulled down low over his face.

"Buttons!" Amber gasped. She couldn't believe her eyes.

The boy on the log pile took off his cap and waved. "'. . . Here we go round the mulberry bush on a cold and frosty morning!'"

7

"I don't get it!" Amber said.

"It's magic!" Buttons laughed as he scrambled down from the log pile.

"No, really!" The boot boy was the last person Amber expected to see, here in the middle of the forest. "Betty said something about her nephew. Is that you?"

Buttons nodded. "That's me – Sir Galahad Buttons, Cinderella's knight in shining armour, at your service!"

"And Betty is your aunt?"

"Right again. Now, Cinders, how was your ride on the grey mare?"

"Bumpy," Amber retorted, rubbing her bruises. She was growing more confused by the second. "How do you know about that?"

"I saw you, didn't I?" Buttons decided it was time to clear things up for Amber. "You don't hear many horses galloping through the streets in the dead of night, so I stole to my window to take a look. And there you were, Cinders – slung like an old carpet across the front of the saddle – bumpety-bump!"

"Wow!" Amber nodded. "That was quick thinking. Then what did you do?"

"Then I went back to bed," Buttons teased. He walked Amber around the clearing, with Bruno playing close by. "No, only joking. I spotted you on Vincent Hunter's grey mare and knew the man was up to no good."

"Vincent Hunter?" For the first time Amber could put a name to her sly, mean kidnapper. "Are you sure?"

Buttons nodded. "I know the villain's horse and I know his boots."

"His boots?"

"Long, black calf leather, with worn-down heels. I clean them for him once a week. The man is a known thief and scoundrel."

"Octavia paid him to kidnap me!" Amber whispered. "He dumped me in the forest and I was meant to starve to death."

"But that's when I stepped in," Buttons explained. "I reckoned Mister Hunter was heading up the mountain into the forest, and, knowing milady Octavia, I guessed what his business might be. So I took a short cut on foot, straight here to Aunt Betty's cottage."

"Buttons woke me up with his hammering at the door," Betty broke in. She called Bruno to come from the house. "Here, boy!"

Bruno came to sit at Amber's feet.

"I told my aunt that we must send Bruno to find you," Buttons went on. "The forest is no place to be alone at night."

Amber crouched to put her arms around the dog's furry neck. "And you did find me," she murmured. "You clever boy!"

"Now, Buttons and Cinderella, come

inside before you catch cold – quick march!" Betty ordered, and she led the way.

They fell in behind – *left-right-left!* – into the warm kitchen.

"This Octavia woman – what should we do about her?" Betty wanted to know.

The sun was rising high in the sky, the cottage windows were open and grey doves flapped across the clearing.

"Put her in prison!" Buttons cried.

"Hush!" Betty told him. She turned to Amber. "Cinderella, my dear, it is not safe for you to go back home, so you may stay here for as long as you wish."

Amber gazed out of the window. She heard the doves cooing and the gentle breeze in the branches. "Thank you, but I have to go back and sort Octavia out."

"Let me do that," Buttons offered. "I'll

go to your house and speak with your father. You can wait here with my aunt."

Amber shook her head. "Thanks, but whatever you told my father, Octavia would wriggle her way out of it. Believe me – I know!"

"Then, if you must see him yourself, rest today and go tomorrow," Betty suggested. "Wait until the Prince's Ball is over at least."

"No, I have to sort this out now." *No one kidnaps me and gets away with it!* Amber thought. She remembered Octavia and the Uglies, the dark shadows and creaking doors. *They can't just chase me and sit on me and send me off to the forest in the dead of night. That's not how it works!*

Buttons tutted. "You see, Aunt, I told

you Cinders was headstrong. The truth is, she wants to get back to town in time to go to the Ball."

"Not me!" Amber cried, folding her arms and jutting out her chin. "I'm not interested in fancy frocks and diamond tiaras. I leave that to Charlotte and Louisa."

"See, she wants to go to the Palace and see the Prince!" Buttons grinned, deliberately winding up Amber.

"Wouldn't every girl?" Betty smiled. "But, Buttons, if Cinderella is set on going back to town, you must go with her. Take her straight to the Palace and tell the Prince's soldiers to arrest this man, Hunter."

"'This is the way we brush our boots,

brush our boots, brush our boots,'"
Buttons chanted. "'This is the way we
brush our boots . . .'" He gave Amber his
broadest grin. "Come on, Cinders, you
know there's a long walk ahead of us."

Left-right, left-right – he marched out of
the cottage.

"Goodbye, Betty," Amber said sadly.
"And goodbye, Bruno!"

The brave dog woofed and wagged
his tail.

"Take great care!" Betty called after
Amber and Buttons as they set off between
the tall trees, down the mountain towards
the town.

8

The gates to the Prince's Palace were tall and wide.

Amber and Buttons stood beside them, peering through the iron bars at a big courtyard and the Palace beyond.

"No visitors today!" a soldier told them. "The Prince won't see anybody. He's too busy getting ready for the Ball."

Servants ran across the courtyard, past

the fountain, carrying pots and pans, chairs and benches. A cart arrived at the gate with yet more chairs. The soldier opened the gates to let the cart in then swiftly closed them again.

"But I was kidnapped!" Amber cried. "We want you to arrest the kidnapper. Plus, I have to talk to the Prince and tell him about Octavia and the Uglies!"

"I'm not arresting anyone today." The soldier tugged at his stiff red tunic. He twirled the edges of his curled moustache. "Tomorrow maybe, though I won't be up early after the Ball. The day after, I expect I'll *definitely* arrest someone."

"B-b-but!" Amber stared. "I've been kidnapped."

The soldier stared back. "Are you sure?

You look to me like a normal girl, free to walk where she pleases."

"I escaped. It was last night!" Amber insisted. "A man in a black cloak came to my house. He galloped off into the forest with me."

"His name is Vincent Hunter," Buttons added.

"Bruno found me and led me to the woodcutter's cottage," Amber rushed on. "He's a St Bernard dog."

"Ha!" the soldier said, as if he'd suddenly seen the joke. "A dog saved your life. Ha-ha, very funny!"

Behind the locked gates, the Prince himself appeared in the palace doorway, surrounded by servants and courtiers with long lists of jobs to be done.

"It's not a joke," Amber insisted. "I wasn't laughing last night when the wolves were howling in the forest and I was alone!"

"Listen, little girl," the soldier said, stooping to Amber's level so that his long, curled moustache almost touched her cheek. "Why don't you stop telling fibs and run along home to get ready for the Ball?

"As for you," he added, turning to Buttons, "I blame you. You're a boy and besides, you're old enough to know better."

"Hey, that's not fair – just because he's a boy and he's older than me!" Amber cried, but Buttons sighed and took her by the arm.

"It's no use," he muttered, leading her

away from the gates.

"It's so not fair!" she said again.

Prince Charming strode slowly across the courtyard as Buttons led Amber away. "Find out what is happening outside the gate," he told a lord with a list.

The lord walked stiffly up to the soldier on duty.

"Forget it," the soldier told the lord with a twirl of his moustache. By now Amber and Buttons were halfway down the hill and not looking back. "Tell His Royal Highness it was nothing – just a silly girl making trouble."

". . . Just a silly girl making trouble," the lord reported back to the Prince.

Prince Charming nodded, though he stared for a while at Amber as she went

73

down the steps. "Order more cakes from the baker," he told a servant. "And bring up more wine from the cellars. Let's make this the biggest and best Ball in the land!"

"Plan number two!" Buttons announced as he sat Amber down on the steps of the fountain in the town's central square.

The whole place bustled with activity. The streets were swept with a hundred

new brooms, flags were raised high on flagpoles.

"Go on, tell me," Amber sighed. She felt like a ship with the wind taken out its sails, flopping about aimlessly on an empty sea. "I don't see what else we can do if we can't get the soldiers to believe us."

"You wait here," Buttons told her. "I'll go off to Vincent Hunter's house, which is just round the corner."

Amber looked up with a start. "What do you want to do that for?"

"For a chat," Buttons said with a wink. "I reckon if I drop a few hints and make it clear that I know what went on at milady Octavia's house last night, Hunter will be forced into a corner and ready to help us out of our difficulty."

"But that's risky!" Amber gasped.

Buttons nodded. "Tell me a better idea."

"I haven't got one. But Vincent Hunter is horrible. What if he turns nasty and tries to kidnap you too?"

"I'll be ready for him," Buttons promised, practising a couple of dodges and shadow punches. "And when I explain to him that there's a reward for talking to your dear old dad, confessing everything and landing Octavia in it, he'll snap my hand off to do it, you'll see."

"Maybe," Amber said slowly. "But I want to come with you, just to make sure."

"You stay here," Buttons said firmly. "You're better out of it. Just give me five minutes and I'll be back, and with any luck I'll have Mister Hunter in tow."

Reluctantly Amber agreed. As Buttons dashed off down a narrow street, she turned and dangled her hot, tired feet in the fountain.

What a night! What a day! She paddled her feet in the cool water. *There's much more to this Cinderella stuff than I ever knew!*

A church bell rang the hour. *Eight-nine-ten-eleven-twelve*. It was midday. The minutes passed. Buttons was longer than he'd thought.

The water from the fountain rose high and splashed down in a million tiny droplets. Through the spray, Amber caught sight of two girls, one tall and thin, the other short and plump, hurrying across the square with shopping bags full

of lace and ribbons, fringed shawls and white kid gloves not three steps from where Amber sat.

"Tonight's the night!" the short one said. "I'm so excited I can hardly breathe!"

Louisa and Charlotte! Amber fell backwards off the fountain ledge in shock. She rolled on the ground then sprang up.

". . . But you must remember, Louisa, that I am to have the first dance with the Prince!" Charlotte was saying in her bossiest voice. Then she saw Amber. ". . . Cinderella!" Her eyes popped.

Louisa looked as if she'd seen a ghost. "Aagh, it can't be . . .!"

"Oh yes it can," Amber muttered. *Unlucky!* she thought. *Of all the people in all this Cinderella world, these are the two I least want to meet!*

The Uglies looked stunned and dropped their bags.

"You-you're supposed to be . . ." Louisa stuttered.

". . . Dead?" Amber asked.

9

"Yeah, well I'm not dead." Amber stood face to face with Charlotte and Louisa. "And soon everyone is going to know about you and your rotten mum!"

"Hush!" Charlotte warned, getting over her surprise. She noticed that a small crowd had gathered. "This is our sister. She's unwell," she explained feebly.

People stared at the Uglies' fine silks and

satins and then at Amber's rags. They shook their heads.

"Our *step*sister," Louisa added sniffily. "Take no notice. Cinderella is as mad as a hatter."

"I'm not crazy and I'm not dead!" Amber protested. "But these two wish I was!"

With this, Charlotte and Louisa made a quick grab for Amber. Charlotte got a bony hand over her mouth, while Louisa seized her round the waist and squeezed. Amber kicked out. This time she wasn't going to let them sit on her and squish the breath out of her.

"Fight!" a kid in the crowd shouted excitedly. He pushed to the front and shadow-boxed. "Hey, ragamuffin girl – try with a left, and now a right to the chin! Who'll bet me a shilling that the girl in the rags wins?"

Amber wrestled her way free. But Louisa ran at her a second time and sent her flying towards the fountain.

As Amber fell, she grabbed at Charlotte's skirt. There was the sound of silk tearing.

"Oh, did you see – she ripped my skirt!" Charlotte wailed as if someone had died. "My poor, poor gown!"

"Vixen!" Louisa cried, coming at Amber again. "I'll teach you to spoil other people's clothes!"

Amber stepped neatly to one side as Louisa charged.

"Whoa!" *Splash!* Louisa was in the

fountain, drenched to the skin.

"Hurray!" the boy in the crowd cheered, and others joined in.

Charlotte ran to help Louisa out of the water. Louisa was too heavy and pulled Charlotte in.

Splash!

"Whoops!" the delighted boy cried.

Both the Uglies sat dripping wet under the fountain.

"Make way!" Someone pushed through from the back of the crowd. It was Buttons, blinking at the messy scene that greeted him.

"I'll explain later," Amber gabbled, grabbing him by the arm. "What happened to you? Where's Hunter?"

"Not at home," Buttons answered. "I searched everywhere. No one knows where he is."

"Except me." A second figure pushed through the crowd – a tall, well-dressed woman in a high wig, her made-up face like a white mask in the bright sunlight.

"Octavia!" Amber and Buttons groaned.

"Mama!" Charlotte and Louisa wailed.

"I've sent Mr Hunter on a short holiday by the seaside," Octavia said in a tight, high voice. She swept forward in her crimson gown. "He rode out of town early this morning."

"Mama, help me!" Louisa cried. "Cinderella shoved me into the water."

"She ripped my dress!" Charlotte added.

"It was an honest fight, two against one, and the ragged girl won fair and square!" the boxing boy exclaimed, before his father hauled him off down the street.

"Don't look so pleased to see me," Amber muttered to Octavia. "I know, you and the Uglies thought I was . . ."

". . . Dead!" Octavia's voice was steely. Her eyes were cold. "That's right. But it seems Mr Hunter couldn't be trusted to carry out the simple task."

"Don't blame him," Amber told her, shaking in her shoes, though she pretended to be brave. Octavia's cruel eyes were seriously scary. "He did his best to get rid of me."

"His best obviously wasn't good enough." Octavia left Charlotte and Louisa to struggle out of the fountain by themselves. "We shall have to try again."

She advanced on Amber, but Buttons stepped between them.

"Scoot!" he ordered Amber. "I'll deal with milady!"

"Scoot where to?" Amber asked. She had nowhere to run, nowhere to hide.

"To your house," he said quickly. "Find your dad. Fly like the wind!"

"Got it!" Amber nodded. She saw the look of fury on Octavia's face. "There's no one there to get in the way. Dad and I can have a proper talk."

"That's right. Go!" Buttons insisted.

Octavia clenched her fists and yelled at

her dripping daughters. "Get out of the water, you little fools! Make haste!"

With a quick nod, Amber ran off across the square. "Thank you!" she yelled over her shoulder at Buttons, who still stood in Octavia's way. "For everything!"

"Father!" Amber had taken the shortest way home. She'd flung open the front doors and raced up the stairs to the old man's library.

In the room lined with books there was no one but the white cat that chased mice from the house.

"Father!" Amber ran along the corridor to his bedroom.

It was empty except for the chambermaid making the bed and

straightening the curtains.

Amber couldn't guess where the old man was. As far as she knew, he never went out of the house.

"Try downstairs in the cellar," the chambermaid told her. "The last I heard he went there looking for you."

"Thanks!" Speeding back along the corridor, Amber flew downstairs two at a time. She ran past the tapestries towards the cellar door.

"Ah, Cinderella, my dear!" The old man stepped out of the cellar with a bemused smile. "I'm glad I've found you."

"Me too!" This was it – Amber's last chance.

"My dear, I've decided I want you to go to the Prince's Ball," Cinders' doddery dad said. "Every young girl is invited, and that includes you. But you must have a new gown."

"Father, it's nice of you to think of me. But I've got something very important to tell you."

"A pretty pink gown with lace and ribbons. And a new blue velvet cloak, and perhaps your poor mother's tiara." He smiled sadly, thinking of his dead wife.

"Father, listen!"

The chambermaid came downstairs. The handle on the front door turned.

"Octavia kidnapped me – honestly and truly, she did!"

The chambermaid gasped and dropped her feather duster. The door opened and there stood Octavia and the Uglies.

"She sent me to the forest to starve!"

". . . A beautiful tiara with diamonds and one as deep as a rose," the old man went on, as if he hadn't even heard Amber's desperate words. "Yes, Cinderella, you shall have your mother's tiara and be the belle of the Ball!"

10

"I have caught my death of cold!" Charlotte complained to Octavia. "Aatchoo!"

"*By dose is rudding!*" Louisa moaned.

"Her nose is running," Charlotte translated. "Send for Cinderella. Tell her to fetch us fresh handkerchiefs this second!"

Amber was locked up in the cellar again. Nothing had changed.

"I refuse to let the wretched girl out of the cellar in case she escapes again," Octavia answered. "You must fetch your own handkerchiefs while I deal with Cinderella's doddery, deluded father!"

Saying this, she went off to the library. "Cinderella will not wear your old wife's diamond tiara," she told her hen-pecked husband. "It will not suit her complexion. Besides, she has tried to drown poor Charlotte and Louisa in the town fountain. I forbid her to go to the Prince's Ball!"

"Very well, my dear," the defeated old man sighed, fixing his glasses on his nose and disappearing behind a leather-bound book.

*

". . . Fe*dge* b*y* ow*b* ha*d*kerchie*ff*!" Louisa spluttered.

"It's an outrage!" Charlotte agreed. "And it's all Cinderella's fault. Come, let's go and punish her!"

"Cinderella!" the Uglies yelled from the top of the cellar steps.

"Not again!" Amber muttered. She sat in the dark with the mice. "Why can't they leave me alone?"

"Come when we call!" Charlotte insisted. She turned the key in the door.

"No, Charlotte!" Louisa protested, her nose suddenly clear. "Mother said we should not let Cinderella out."

"We're not letting her out," Charlotte answered crossly. "We're going to punish her."

Want to bet? Amber thought. Looking up, she saw the Uglies' feet and skirts at the top of the steps. Quickly she grabbed her old bonnet from the table and jammed it on her head, ready to race up the stairs and knock them over before she charged for the front door.

"Uh-oh, Mama's coming!" Louisa gasped, tugging Charlotte back out of the cellar.

The cellar door slammed shut. The key turned.

Lucky for you! Amber thought, picturing what she would have done to them this time. A quick elbow in Charlotte's skinny ribs, a hefty shove to send Louisa sprawling down the hallway . . .

But Amber hadn't had time to act. With

a big sigh she sat down by the glowing grate. "As for this old thing!" she muttered, seizing the bonnet and throwing it angrily into the fire where the dry straw flared and burned. "This is how it all started – with that silly old hat!"

Red sparks rose up the chimney. Amber felt the heat of the dancing flames.

In a burst of sudden orange and silver light, a fairy appeared.

"Cinderella, it is high time to get you ready for the Ball!" the fairy godmother tinkled in a silvery voice.

"I told you – I don't want to go!" Amber cried. What had brought this on? Why had Fairy G showed up a second time?

"Stuff and nonsense!" The fairy's voice

sounded like a tiny silver bell. "Every girl wants to go to the Ball. You have your satin gown. Now you must have your diamond tiara."

"It was the magic hat!" Amber realised. She saw the flames from the bonnet die down and its wispy ashes float up the chimney.

"You must not be late if you are to have the first dance with Prince Charming," the fairy insisted as she tiptoed around Amber and waved her magic wand.

Amber's ragged skirt changed in an instant into the beautiful pink ball gown trimmed with pearls and lace.

Whoosh! Fairy G waved again. A cloud of silver light filled the room.

Amber's hands flew up to her head.

She felt a tiara perched in her smooth blonde hair.

"Take it off," the fairy told her. "Look at it. See how it shines!"

So Amber took off the tiara and saw that it was studded with twinkling diamonds. In the centre was a deep pink, precious ruby to set off the pale pink ribbons of her gown. "Oh!" she gasped in delight. "But listen – you don't understand. I'm not exactly who you think I am!"

"Tut-tut, Cinderella!" the fairy scolded. "We don't have time to talk."

"B-but!" Amber stammered. The gown was lovely. The tiara sparkled brighter than the droplets in the fountain.

"Put your tiara back on," the fairy godmother ordered. "Fluff out your petticoats. Straighten your hair."

Amber did as she was told.

"Perfect!" the fairy said with a bright smile. "Turn around, Cinderella. Let me look at you before I order a carriage to take you to the Ball!"

Amber turned with the glittering tiara perched on her head. The room grew bright. She felt dizzy, so she closed her eyes and began . . . to . . . yes, she began to float!

"Here she comes!" Pearl cried.

Amber's fingers grasped the sides of the dressing-up box. Her head emerged from a heap of old clothes.

Lily gasped. "She was hidden in there all this time!"

"Look at what she's wearing." Pearl pointed to Amber's glittery diamond tiara.

"Amber, get out of there quick!" Lily insisted, running to help.

The tiara wobbled and fell forward over Amber's forehead.

"Wow, they look like real diamonds!" Pearl snatched the tiara and admired it. "And a real ruby – wowee!"

"Amber, Pearl, Lily – did you find my hat?" Amber's mum asked as she came down the stairs into the basement.

Amber staggered out of the dressing-up

box in her pink satin gown. "Not yet!" she called back.

"Here it is – at last!" Lily seized a wide-brimmed hat from the box.

Pearl put Amber's tiara back on her head. "You look cool!" she grinned. "Come on, Amber, give us a twirl!"

But Amber refused. "No more twirls!" she vowed, "not ever again!"

And she took the gardening hat from Lily and ran to give it to her mum.

A sneak peek at Amber's next adventure:

The Velvet Cloak

"I'm going to a fancy dress party but I don't know what to wear," Pearl told Amber and Lily.

"Come and look in my dressing-up box," Amber suggested.

The three girls ran down to Amber's basement.

"Where's the satin dress?" Lily asked Amber. "You know – the pretty pink one that you wore before."

"And the princess tiara?" Pearl added.

"Oh, those old things!" Amber was trying to forget the magic twirls and dazzle that had swept her into a dream world. "Here, Pearl – try this fairy costume. It was a Christmas present from my gran."

Pearl tried on the white frilly dress. She turned on the spot. "It's creased," she said. "I'd like something sparkly, with sequins and stuff."

"You're not expecting much!" Amber said, rummaging deep in the box. She came up with her mum's old party dress.

"Pink sequins!" Lily grabbed the dress and held it up against Pearl. "Cool!"

Pearl tried it on while Amber rummaged

again. This time she came up with a dusty black cloak.

"Yuck, that's whiffy!" Lily told her. "Throw it away!"

But Amber had other ideas. She wrapped the cloak around her. "I'm the Wicked Witch of the West!" she cackled.

"Get lost, Amber!" Pearl cried. The pink sequins suited her. She'd found her perfect dress.

"I'm the wicked witch!" Amber chanted, raising her arms and spinning round.

A cloud of dust rose from the cloak. It began to glitter gold and silver.

"Stop, Amber, you're choking us!" Lily coughed.

Amber kept on spinning. Lily's voice faded. There was a dazzling light.

Have you checked out...

www.dressingupdreams.net

It's the place to go for games, downloads, activities, sneak previews and lots of fun!

You'll find a special dressing-up game and lots of activities and fun things to do, as well as news on Dressing-Up Dreams and all your favourite characters.

Sign up to the newsletter at **www.dressingupdreams.net** to receive extra clothes for your Dressing-Up Dreams doll and the opportunity to enter special members only competitions.

What happens next...?
Log onto www.dressingupdreams.net for a sneak preview of my next adventure!

WIN A Dressing-Up Dreams GOODIE BAG!

CAN YOU SPOT THE TWO DIFFERENCES AND THE HIDDEN LETTER IN THESE TWO PICTURES OF AMBER?

There is a spot-the-difference picture and hidden letter in the back of all four Dressing-Up Dreams books about Amber (look for the books with to 4 on the spine). Hidden in one of the pictures above is a secret letter. Find all four letters and put them together to make a special Dressing-Up Dreams word, then send it to us. Each month, we will put the correct entries in a draw and one lucky winner will receive a magical Dressing-Up Dreams goodie bag including an exclusive Dressing-Up Dreams keyring!

Send your magical word, your name and your address
on a postcard to: **The Dressing-Up Dreams Competition**

UK Readers:
Hodder Children's Books
338 Euston Road
London NW1 3BH
smarketing@hodder.co.uk

Australian Readers:
Hachette Children's Books
Level 17/207 Kent Street
Sydney NSW 2000
childrens.books@hachette.com.au

New Zealand Readers:
Hachette Livre NZ Ltd
PO Box 100 749
North Shore City 0745
childrensbooks@hachette.co.nz

Only one entry per child. Final draw: 27th February 2009
For full terms and conditions go to www.hachettechildrens.co.uk/terms

COLOURING FUN!

Carefully colour the Dressing-Up Dreams picture on the next page and then send it in to us.

Or you can draw your very own fairytale character. You might want to think about what they would wear or if they have special powers.

Each month, we will put the best entries on the website gallery and one lucky winner will receive a magical Dressing-Up Dreams goodie bag!

Send your drawing, your name and
your address on a postcard to:
The Dressing-Up Dreams Competition

UK Readers:	**Australian Readers:**	**New Zealand Readers:**
Hodder Children's Books	Hachette Children's Books	Hachette Livre NZ Ltd
338 Euston Road	Level 17/207 Kent Street	PO Box 100 749
London NW1 3BH	Sydney NSW 2000	North Shore City 0745
kidsmarketing@hodder.co.uk	childrens.books@hachette.com.au	childrensbooks@hachette.co